Cocoons and Cases

Kim Wilson

Rigby

What's in here?

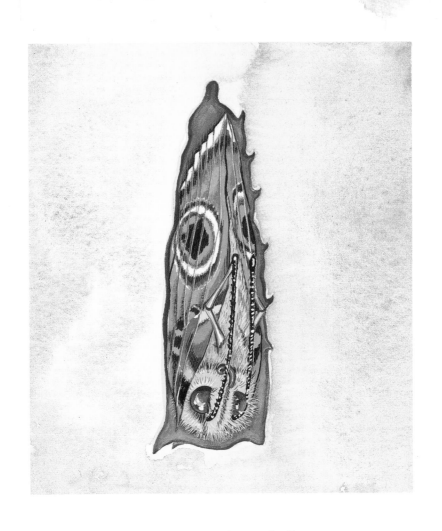

What is it?

It's a butterfly.

What is it?

It's a bee.

What's in here?

What's in here?

It's an ant.

What's in here?

It's a wasp.

What's in here?

It's a moth.

What's in here?

It's a fly.

Life cycle of a butterfly

Index